Lee Aucoin, *Creative Director*
Jamey Acosta, *Senior Editor*
Heidi Fiedler, *Editor*
Produced and designed by
Denise Ryan & Associates
Illustration © Abigail Marble
Rachelle Cracchiolo, *Publisher*

Teacher Created Materials
5301 Oceanus Drive
Huntington Beach, CA 92649-1030
http://www.tcmpub.com
Paperback: ISBN: 978-1-4333-5561-5
Library Binding: ISBN: 978-1-4807-1706-0
© 2014 Teacher Created Materials

In a Whirl

Written by Helen Bethune

Illustrated by Abigail Marble

When I grow up, I want to work with animals. There are lots of ways to do that. So I played a game with my globe. I whirled it very fast. Then, I closed my eyes and stopped it with my finger. It landed in the middle of the ocean!

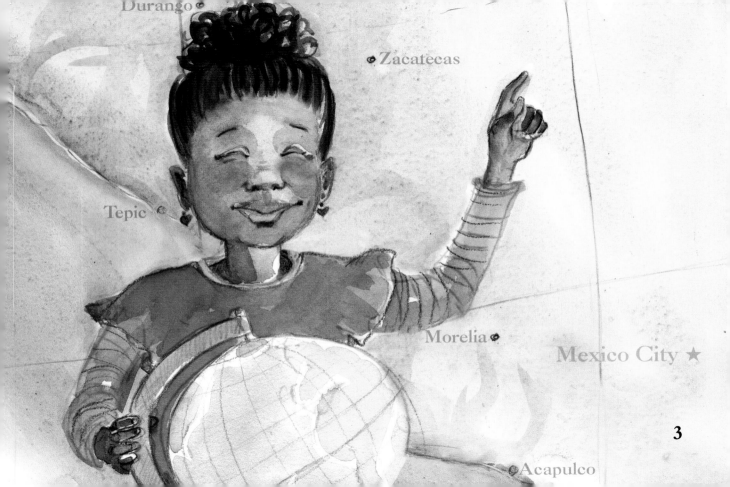

Durango

Zacatecas

Tepic

Morelia

Mexico City ★

Acapulco

3

I thought really hard about that. What could a scientist do there? Then, I remembered a program I saw on TV. It was about scientists who work with sea animals. It was amazing! Maybe, I could be a marine biologist. They look for rare sea creatures and collect data.

The ocean is so deep it has been divided into zones.
Most sea creatures live in the top zone. That's because
they need light. I would love to go swimming there.
I could swim with dolphins, turtles, and coral!

6

Maybe I could dive down to the next zone.
The deeper you are, the less light there is. The fish have
huge eyes so they can find food. They look weird and
a bit scary.

If I went even deeper, there wouldn't be any light at all. The deepest parts of the ocean are totally black and very cold. The ocean floor is covered with ooze. Yuck!

The ocean is too cold. And it's too dark! I won't work there!

I whirled the globe again. I opened my eyes slowly. This time, my finger pointed at the Mojave Desert. What could I study in the desert?

12

I had no idea, so I looked it up online. Wow! Part of the Mojave Desert is almost like the surface of Mars. Astronauts even go there to study what it might be like to live on Mars. But what sort of creatures live in the desert?

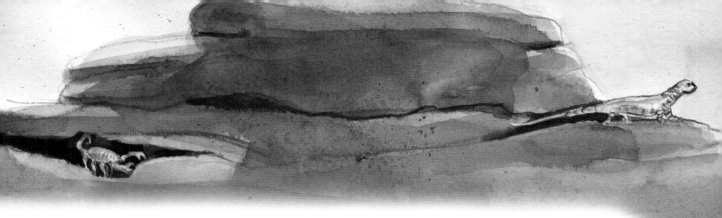

I read more data about deserts. Insects and reptiles live in sandy deserts. Those deserts don't have rain. They can be very hot during the day. They can be very cold at night.

The desert is too hot. And it's too cold. And I don't like any of the creatures that live there!

GALAPAGOS ISLANDS

FERNANDINA

ISAI

I whirled the globe again. This time my finger landed near the Galapagos Islands. They are just off the coast of South America. Those islands are awesome! My family went there last year.

SANTIAGO

A

BALTRA

SANTA CRUZ

SANTA FE

19

Scientists think the Galapagos Islands have never been joined to any other area of land. So the creatures that live there can't be found anywhere else in the world.

There are amazing animals there. Crabs! Seals! And what I really like are the tortoises! There used to be lots of them.

23

But not any more. Long ago, people took many tortoises away from the islands. Then, settlers brought farm animals. Those animals ate the eggs and killed the hatchlings.

Goats and donkeys ate the plants. There was no food for the tortoises. So some types of tortoises became extinct. Now, scientists are raising young hatchlings at the research station. They are helping the tortoises survive.

I know! I could work at the research station! I could help protect the new tortoises.

(Funny. I thought of that before. Guess I forgot.)